RISE

INSPIRATIONAL, REAL-LIFE POEMS FOR
YOUNG ADULTS IN PURSUIT OF PERSONAL DEVELOPMENT

ENIOLA OLUWASOROMIDAYO

Syncterface Media
London
www.syncterfacemedia.com

The right of Eniola Oluwasoromidayo to be identified as the author of the work has been asserted by her in accordance with the Copyright, Designs and Patents Act, 1988.

All rights reserved.
No part of this publication may be reproduced, stored in a retrieval system, or transmitted in any form or by any means, electronic, mechanical, photocopying, recording or otherwise without prior written permission of the publisher, or in the case of reprographic reproduction in accordance with the terms of licences issued by the Copyright Licensing Agency.

All names have been changed to protect the privacy of individuals.

Enquiries concerning reproduction outside these terms should be sent to
eniolaoluwasoromidayo@gmail.com

RISE
Inspirational, Real-Life Poems For
Young Adults in Pursuit of Personal Development

ISBN: 978-1-912896-31-8
Copyright © June 2022
Eniola Oluwasoromidayo
All Rights Reserved

Published in the United Kingdom by

SYNCTERFACE™
Syncterface Media, London
www.syncterfacemedia.com
info@syncterfacemedia.com

Cover Concept by Rebecca-Ira

British Library Cataloguing in Publication Data
A catalogue record for this book is available from the British Library

To the young people in care or leaving care and the professionals who work with children, families, and young people

Acknowledgements

I would like to thank Lanre Iroche, Ben Swift, Mark Nasha and Bunmi Olubode for their support in making this book a reality.

Above all, I want to thank my best friend, God Almighty, the Father of my Lord Jesus Christ, who is the bedrock of my faith.

a word from The Author

I have had the privilege of supporting young people during good and challenging times. In life, unexpected setbacks happen to us all, yet, while our stories may or may not be similar, our reactions to the trauma vary from person to person.

This book is about confronting mental conflicts and vulnerabilities and the choices we make based on our beliefs, emotions, attitudes, and actions while pursuing personal development.

It is okay to feel emotionally challenged sometimes – what you feel is being human; it is common to us all. However, that should not be your permanent state.

This book has been written to bring comfort and activate your strength, to motivate you to enjoy life and fulfil your potential to the fullest. This wisdom for living has been shared to supplement your support system however limited it may be in terms of family or friends. Any adult going through difficult times might also find this book beneficial. Please seek help if you need further emotional support.

Professionals can also use this book as a tool to foster topics for discussion, especially when a young person struggles to name their emotions or verbalise the impact of a particular challenge on their mental health.

Someone described this book as being like a friend you can carry around. I hope you enjoy reading it and that each word will inspire strength, hope and fortitude.

Contents

Copyright ii
Dedication iii
Acknowledgements v
A Word from the Author vi

INSPIRATIONAL, REAL-LIFE POEMS AND PROSE FOR YOUNG ADULTS IN PURSUIT OF PERSONAL DEVELOPMENT

Do You Know My Story? 1
Worry 5
Choice Factory 8
Dream 10
Career 12
Life's Trial 16
Will You Tell My Story? 18
Give Me A Reason To Live 20
Me! Don't Give Up On Me 22
My You (My Body) Suffers 24
Discrimination,... Like A Milk Allergy 26
A Thread Of Hope 28
Friends 29
What Is Betrayal? 32
Rain 35
Oil Of Truth 36
Forgive 37
One-Member Family 39
Use Your Grief 42
Uniqueness 44

Busyness	45
Forced Marriage	47
My Partner	48
What Do You Do?	50
Variety In Life	52
The Love Of My Unborn Children	55
Negatives	57
Words	59
Conscientious Awareness	61
I Find	63

POEMS DEDICATED TO RAISING AWARENESS FOR INVISIBLE DISABILITY

Every Disability Matters	65
Employed & Disabled ~ I Can't Breathe!	67

POEMS DEDICATED TO MY COLLEAGUES IN SOCIAL SERVICES

Looked After Children and Leaving Care Team ~ Team Unusual	72
Dean at 50! Who Is Dean?	74
Jane The Water	76
A Foster Carer	78
Who Is AKM?	79
A Letter To Coronavirus	80
Conclusion	85
About The Author	86

Inspirational,
Real-Life Poems for
Young Adults
in Pursuit of
Personal Development

Do You Know My Story?

Here is a piece that deals with the assumptions people make regardless of knowing the whole story or not. We all fall victim to judging people without knowing the full extent of their story, and I believe that these words will resonate with anyone going through tough times. To be resilient in the face of judgment is key, so I like this one.

Do You Know My Story?
If you don't know my story,
be careful not to condemn me
for my slightest frailty;

If you don't know my story,
be cautious not to write me off
at the first glimpse of my mistakes;

If you don't know my story,
be mindful not to be insensitive
to the faint cry for help echoing from my narrative;

If you don't know my story,
beware not to talk me down
at the discovery of my vulnerability,
or when you find that I did not apply wisdom
to certain situations in my life and acted naively.

Do You Know My Story?
If you don't know my story,
careful not to be too quick to think for me
and make a decision without my views;

If you don't know my story,
be cautious not to label me as oversensitive
for standing up for myself,
as my reactions might be reflective of being prey to the negative
experiences that I have overcome;

If you don't know my story,
be mindful not to disrespect me
when I need a shoulder to lean on and an ear to listen;

If you don't know my story,
beware not to dismiss my actions,
I only know the triggers to my responses;

If you don't know my story,
be careful not to act as an expert
in making my decisions for me,
for only I will face the consequences of such decisions.

Do You Know My Story?
When I turn to addictions to cope
with my life's pain and sorrow;
In a bid to save my mind from thinking about my problems,
you come along and label me a spoilt brat.

The idea is, all these things I do and struggle with
may ultimately become an addiction,
but still, that does not give you the right to label me
a spoilt brat without knowing my story.

RISE

When I underachieve academically
because my foundation for studying has been affected
by a family breakdown so much so that
I keep struggling to catch up with my peers,
And nothing seems to materialise within the desired time frame
even after putting in a lot of hard work;

When I disguise my pain with a smile
and hide my disappointment due to life's failures,
or hide away from my friends and family
who can easily know when something is wrong with me;

Or am afraid to have a blank mind,
thus keeping myself too busy to avoid thinking,
or unsure how I am feeling due to
numbness, sadness, and disappointment.

Do You Know My Story?
When life's challenges overflow and I don't seem to know
how and when I will move past them,
or when people advise me to settle for less
due to my repeated failures,
forgetting that trying again could result in success;

When I help others whilst I am silently suffering,
too ashamed to speak out,
or ask for help for fear of being judged or labelled;
I feel life is passing me by, and I'm powerless to do something.

Listen!
Out of my pain and disappointment came courage,
hope, resilience, hard work, strength, and determination;
Out of my vulnerability and helplessness emerged
the passion to be an advocate for the voiceless.

Out of my weakness,
which had once overshadowed my strength,
I have become an icon that stands for restoration,
reminding others that there is a second chance.

Out of my life of challenges, failures,
disappointments, and mistakes
arose a necessity for survival and growth,
And out of my suffering came
the desire to impact others positively.

Even If you know my story,
be careful not to condemn my conclusion on matters;
You only know as much as I have revealed to you.

Even if you know my story,
All of the above still applies to you!

Worry

Worry is a feeling that we all harbour. It restricts us from chasing our dreams; it paralyses us with the fear of anxiety, shutting out some of the most intuitive minds. I think this poem resonates with me because "worry" goes hand-in-hand with trauma. It can destroy your self-esteem and make you feel like never trying again when you fail. But failure is more of a lesson than an absolute conclusion. This poem will encourage you to deal with worry healthily and regulate it so that it doesn't restrict you from achieving your potential.

Worry,
How could you be so callous after all I did for you?
You were homeless, and I offered you a sanctuary in my mind
Little did I know that your goal was to invade
and turn it into your playground,
a laboratory where you experimented with your tricks;
Now I know your feelings towards me,
so I seek the wisdom to rid you completely.

O Worry,
Where is your face?
What new tricks have you got under your sleeve?
You came into my life, appearing as a friend,
and I welcomed you, believing we had things in common
Only to discover that your counsel was aimed
at making me fearful, paralysing my hopes of dreaming again.

If I had known,
I would have sent you away
the moment you came,
pretending to care.

I hear of deadly diseases with no cure,
but my experience with you suggests that
you are worse than any of those,
worse than an airborne disease that creeps in.

Please, you friends of *Worry*,
before you judge me and fight for *Worry's* right to live,
check the statistics of his club members
And while you're at it, check the state of their health.

Worry,
Some have grown tired of you;
some have retired, others have committed suicide,
and some are on their way to illness.

O Worry,
You are a companion with no benefits;
I think about how to get rid of you,
but you frighten me by shutting my eyes to everything
but negative possibilities.

You subject me to hopelessness
with your false reports and records;
You portray death as an honourable escape from
the pressures of fighting for my dream;

You make me feel irrelevant
and insist that my talents and skills are outdated,
that I will never contribute to the world's advancement.

I am now following a moment-by-moment approach
to dispel you from my life, my mind, and my body;
I know it will be hard,
but I am ready to begin that journey,
TODAY!

Choice Factory

Perfect! This one is a favourite of mine as it shows you are accountable. It reverts to the first poem about judgement. So many factors influence one's decisions, but to everyone, you will always be the face of your actions. So, hold yourself accountable before anyone else can.

The choices you make help shape the nature of your decisions,
The nature of your decisions shapes your actions and reactions,
Your actions and reactions shape the outcomes of your life,
Your life reflects the right and wrong choices you have made.

The information used to make choices cannot be blamed,
even though they help you reach an informed decision.
You and you alone are accountable for your decisions,
You and your feelings dictate making the decisions.
You are the face of the decisions you make,
And not your feelings or your circumstances.

So, think about the impact of your choices
before making them;
Don't be governed by hormones, emotions, or feelings,
They are faceless partners who won't accept the blame
if things go wrong.

In the choice factory,
you are accountable for your own choices.
So, think deep, not shallow,
Expand your knowledge through research, not rumours,
Avoid blaming negative emotions to justify your actions.

At the end of the day,
Only you will be responsible for the choices you make
Only you will live with them
So, make the right choices.

Dream

I like this poem as it relates to today's modern standards. Everyone wants to have success around the same time their family and peers get it. However, it is not a linear path; many ups and downs can occur. I think younger people will relate, especially as social media portrays many young people as super successful and happy. In turn, some become depressed as they witness the success of people their age or younger. This poem shows that you should wait for the right time and seize your opportunity when it comes.

The dream never dies!
Only the perseverance towards achieving it.
Dreams, although invisible,
are dependent on you for their survival.

You should try and protect it,
Help it grow and flourish into reality;
Not all setbacks are bad,
Some are also paths that lead to your next step.

Breakthroughs are like your everyday journeys,
Sometimes you take the bus,
Other times, you take the train and travel faster,
Occasionally, you get on a plane, which is even quicker.

But, whichever mode you use,
it is designed to get you to your destination.

The road towards breakthrough is filled with stops
So, be careful not to miss yours.

At some stops,
you'll find people willing to jump-start your vehicle,
At others, you'll find someone ready to repair it,
While others will drive alongside you to your destination.
Then you can share your dream with the world
To make someone else's dream come true.

Career

This poem acts as an anthology of mistakes and missteps that might happen when forming a career for yourself. It is always good to retrospectively look at what was done wrong. This poem shows you some of the mistakes that can happen from the author's perspective. It is apt for anyone starting their career as it is akin to a mini rule-book on what to do and what not to do.

Career progression depends on determination,
and so does career stagnation.

Sometimes, there is a thin line between
an experienced applicant and an inexperienced one,
that is, access to opportunity.

Having a dream is abstract,
but achieving your dream is practical.

Procrastination bears no fruit,
but taking action is a fruitful effort.

Opportunities are uncontrollable,
but preparations are intentional.

Laziness is a choice,
but hard work has rewarding outcomes.

Wishing is a mirage,
taking steps is the real deal.

Accountability leads to maturity,
whereas making excuses is obstructive.

Vision is direction,
and no ambition signals a labyrinth.

Excellent output is distinct,
while the standard forms the crowd.

Success is an advert,
No one individual is an island of knowledge.

Avoid perceiving the harshness of one as the harshness of all,
Otherwise, you'll lose your opportunities for growth.

Your critics' success does not indicate
their superiority over you,
Your time of success will come

Attributing the shortcomings of a few to everyone
only births a judgmental mindset.

The easiest path to loneliness is shutting others out.

You can't always have your way when working with others,
so better partner with others.

Be the one who prevents conflict,
not the one who instigates it.

Clarifying the information you give
prevents errors and mistakes,
Not clarifying could jeopardise your hard work.

You don't have control over time,
but you do have control over what you do with yours.

There is no greater freedom than being yourself,
even amidst people with expectations of you

Avoid living for people's approval,
The same mouth that once praised
can condemn you when things don't go their way.

First-hand learning serves you for life.

Sometimes, in quietness and isolation lies creative thinking.

Your position's relevance to people's needs
determines the number of people you influence.

You can pay people to do the work,
but you can't make them care about the work.

Seek someone willing to go out of their way for you;
avoid expecting or demanding favours.

You cannot demand another's time by being rude,
even if you are paying for it.

Integrity has a price,
it is called an honest and disciplined lifestyle.

Life's Trials

Comparing life's challenges to everyday things shows how everyone in this world, regardless of status, deals with life's trials and tribulations. When you are going through issues, it can feel unique and personal to the point that you think no one will understand. However, this feeling of doubt and depression is something everyone will go through at some or many points in their lives.

Life's trials are like the wind;
You get to experience them,
but no one can be held accountable for them,
Yet you feel pain and sorrow in your bone and marrow.

Life's trials are like a recession;
With the prices rising
and the hopes of their decrease slowly fading,
You get used to the constant increase.

Life's trials are like the height of a human being;
Your growth stops all of a sudden,
And you wonder what has befallen you.

Life's trials are like expectant mothers;
Nine months feel like forever,
but the tiredness of waiting vanishes
the second you see your child for the first time.

Life's trials are like courses you enrol in;
From first breath to first step,
you constantly move to the next challenge,
And they continue until you graduate;
When you breathe your last breath

Life's trials are like necessities;
Like air and water, you cannot live without them,
They ensure your sustenance.

Life's trials are the greatest gift;
They make you mature and independent;
Above all, they help you discover yourself.

Will You Tell My Story?

Now, here is a solid tale about giving a voice to the voiceless – who will know why I behave the way I behave and the actions I undertook were not in vain?

Will you tell my story...
When I have fought and am tired of fighting?

Will you tell my story...
When delay has got my motivation bound?

Will you tell my story...
When the evidence of my hard work is unseen?

Will you tell my story...
When all options make me feel like a failure
and I give up on my dreams?

Will you tell my story...
When the alternative chosen leaves me betraying myself, ruining
all prior work?

Will you tell my story...
When my refusal to make things right might label me lazy?

Will you tell my story...
When they stand against me because they believe a lie?

Will you tell my story...
When I'm weak,
but even in my weakness, I refuse to give up,
Even when my strength fails to lift me?

Will you tell my story...
That I would rather keep aiming for the best
than settle for less?

Will you tell my story...
If my lips are paralysed, and I can't tell my own story?
Of how I remained hopeful till the end
and never gave up?

Will you tell my story...
That life is hard,
but I am harder on life by not giving up?

Give Me A Reason To Live

*This poem relates to anyone who has experienced depression and/or suicidal thoughts. It is easy, once you have repetitively told yourself that you are not worth anything, to find the negative in everything humanly possible. Feeling depressed but not suicidal can be linked to past trauma that seems inescapable. When you feel suicidal, it's a culmination of telling yourself, 'You are not worth it' and 'People would be better off without me.' The line **'the light might seem dim, I can still see your wonders in my life'** shows that although you may feel some way, others may not see you in the same darkness you see yourself in.*

Give me a reason to live.
It's not that I want to die,
but I don't want to just take up space.
I want my life to matter, to change lives
including those of future generations;
To make this world a better place to live.
So, give me a reason to live.

I see my life full of struggles,
With every achievement, twenty setbacks;
Does this mean my God has abandoned me?

RISE

My Bible tells me 'No',
My spirit tells me 'No',
But my flesh remains unsure.
Which of these should my thoughts dwell on?
God, give me the strength to dwell on you.

I am exhausted but not ready to end my race.
I want to keep running, but I fear I will fail.
So, give me the strength to carry your torch
Though the light might seem dim,
I can still see your wonders in my life,
So, give me a reason to live.

---

*This poem will not apply to everyone,
but if you are experiencing suicidal thoughts or contemplating suicide, please seek help.*

Me! Don't Give Up On Me!

This poem is vital as it shows that giving up is the easier route in the short term; you will have less workload and more idle time. However, in the long term, you will be burdened with the thought of 'what could have been if you had persevered and seen it to the end. It doesn't matter if you fail. At least you can say you tried and gave it your all. I like how optimism is not unrealistic. Yes, you will go through some hard and testing times, but the reward is worth the risk.

Life challenges are tough,
but you can be tougher by not giving up on yourself.

Setbacks, rejections, and unfair treatment are stops,
but the pursuit of your dream conquers them all.

Failure will delay or slow down
the achievement of your dreams,
but trying again and achieving it
will make up for the lost time.

The high turnover of rejection
will try and force you to give up,
but the thirst for your dream will carry you forward.

Giving up is easy,
achieving is hard work.

RISE

Seeing the possibility of your dream
will encourage you to aim higher;
Expand your imagination!

Forgetting what it's like to be successful is attainable,
but living without trying your best to achieve your dream
is unbearable.

Settling for less makes my skin crawl,
as well as knowing I can do better but refusing to try.

I dare you to try!
In trying, you will shed tears, groan, get hurt,
be overwhelmed, feel tired and burnt out,
but on the day your dream comes true
you'll feel the price is worth the crown.

I say, fight with every drop of blood in your vein,
Pick courage as your partner and zeal as your friend;
Don't forget to have fun as you fight,
You will need it to cheer you up when you get stressed

Above all, I wish you all the best.

This poem will not apply to everyone,
but if you are experiencing low moods or depression, please seek help.

My You (My Body) Suffers

This poem deals with the idea of mental health and the physical ramifications that can happen due to it. The mind can play negative tricks on you, which can harm the body and your general health.

My ever-present, *you*
My ever-submissive twin
My body sharer,
My voiceless version
My best friend
My close companion
As I grow, you grow
As I dance, you dance
As I cry, you cry.

We simultaneously eat, sleep, and walk;
You have known and witnessed my life story,
And we do everything together
Yet, I am the one with the gift of a voice.
We were born together as one, inseparable,
Yet, nature gave me more control over you.

Sometimes,
You express your views and wishes through cravings,
And sometimes
I silence you through self-control.

RISE

When I refuse to eat, being in a low mood, you suffer,
When I decide to self-harm, you suffer,
When I give up on myself, you suffer,
When I let others take advantage of me, you suffer,
When I turn to substance or alcohol abuse, you suffer,
When I believe the lies of others
and decide to give up on my life goals, you suffer,
When I experience constant insomnia because of stress,
You suffer.

I am sorry for when I tried to end it all,
When there seemed no light at the end of the tunnel;
I am sorry for all the negative choices I've made,
You've had to share the consequences of my decisions;
I promise to always try and consider the impact of my actions
on you before I carry them out.

When I fight for you,
You will be proud and glad
that I stood for what was right.

Thank you for always being there for me,
even when I don't deserve you;
You, my twin, my body!
YOU!

This poem will not apply to everyone,
but if you are self-harming or contemplating harming yourself, please seek help.

Discrimination,...
Like A Milk Allergy

This poem shows that in a world full of people with conflicting views and opinions, you can clash with colleagues and superiors. The author likens it to having an allergy. Regardless of how much you try to change or alter the perception of these people, they will react in the same way allergies react – indiscriminately. The ultimate message here is that, in the aftermath of trying to work through it and all other options, we should seek a change in company or career. This is important as sometimes, no matter how much you try to make it work, the cause of this discrimination may be due to deep-rooted issues.

Discrimination is like
being allergic to a specific milk product.

There are different types of milk,
and you might not be allergic to them all;
You might like to drink dairy milk
but it might not like you back,
hence the allergies you experience
when it gets into your system.

Similarly, a particular supervisor might be
the dairy milk that you're allergic to;
You may do your best in your job to get along
yet still be excluded because of what you represent.

RISE

Never blame yourself for being discriminated against,
It is not your fault!

Remember that you cannot force your allergy to accept you,
it will only cause further harm to your body.
The same is true of the supervisor
who makes you feel excluded
or discriminates against you.

Instead of trying to make the dairy milk accept you,
I suggest you try out another kind of milk, such as:
Rice milk, Coconut milk, Oats milk,
Soya milk, Almond milk, Cashew nut milk,
Peanut milk, Walnut milk, Organic milk,...

Keep looking until you find the one
suitable for your consumption.
Likewise, keep applying to other departments or organisations
till you find the one that truly accepts and supports you.

Just like a fish has been created to live in water,
and a bird to fly in the sky,
and just like some animals live on land,
you, too will hopefully find your own career habitation
where you can soar and flourish.

This poem will not apply to everyone.
However, if you have experienced discrimination at work and it has impacted your well-being,
please seek help.

A Thread Of Hope

An optimistic poem that shows that we can hold onto that thread of hope that we can spin into a sheet of positive outcomes and milestones even in the darkest of times. When facing a sea of negativity, it's good to think of the positives that have happened in the past.

A thread of hope made me believe in myself,
A thread of hope encouraged me to seek help,
A thread of hope persuaded me
to accept the love and care of others,
A thread of hope carried me to the shower,
A thread of hope made me beautiful,
A thread of hope gave me comfort,
A thread of hope wiped away my tears,
A thread of hope helped me fall asleep,
A thread of hope made me smile,
A thread of hope gave me inspiration,
A thread of hope freed me to make friends again,
A thread of hope helped me forgive,
A thread of hope made me accept myself
and others for themselves,
A thread of hope made me laugh,
A thread of hope pushed me to fight for myself,
A thread of hope made me dream again.
I love you, my thread of hope.

Friends

It acts as a rule book for the young and vulnerable that the choice of who you call your friend can dictate what the future holds for you. Although you could be intelligent and capable, friends can lead you in negative and positive directions. Hence, it is very important to be cautious of who you pick.

Avoid trusting someone who consistently undermines you;
Avoid revealing your weaknesses to those quick to condemn;
Avoid relying on a friend
who is only accessible at their convenience;
Avoid an exploiter in your time of need,
they will only prey on your desperation.

Avoid seeking someone who loves what you hate,
you will eventually regret it;
Avoid trusting someone who often cuts corners,
they might do the same to you;
Avoid judging a friend by their finished work,
judge them by their commitment to honesty,
integrity, and transparency;
Avoid seeking a partnership
where what you bring is redundant.

A friend who keeps records of your failures
stands at the floodgates of doubt;

Avoid absorbing negativity
by spending time with someone who breeds it;
Friends who advise you to pursue ways contrary to the best
reveal their true convictions;
Anyone who compromises their values to be with you
will do the same when they are with you;
Where you find greed,
there is often disobedience and manipulation.

Consideration for others can always be seen
in the little things,
Watch out for the little things;
Test people with little try-outs
before entrusting them with big tasks;
Take heed of any advice from someone who has lost hope;
Just as a smile is infectious,
so is keeping an ill-mannered friend for company.

Someone else's goodwill might open a door for you,
but only your character will keep you in the room;
Politeness will gain you favour,
whereas rudeness will isolate you;
Your self-worth reveals itself in the decisions you make;
It doesn't matter where you were born or as who,
It matters that you provide things for others to live on;
What you stand for in life
will constitute the legacy you leave behind.

Things and people are not always as they appear,
Beware of the mirages your emotions sometimes create;

RISE

The best indicator of your resilience
manifests during your trials,
Those who walk with you then are the ones who value you;
Whoever sticks with you when you have nothing
will watch your back when you have something;
If you must be someone else for someone else's benefit,
then they are not worth your friendship;
Always be yourself!

If someone is important to you,
show it through your actions,
They will believe your words thereafter.

Assumption is the prime source of conflict and strife,
As is overfamiliarity with people you've just met,
a door to suspicion.

Identifying the root of your perception
will help change negative mindsets.

Trust is the foundation for agreements,
And in the multitude of agreements lies confidence.

A real friend covers another's shame,
A real friend is hard to come by,
so hold on tight when you've found one;
Celebrate the people you want to share joy with,
and vice versa.

What Is Betrayal?

Everyone experiences betrayal of some sort. Whether it is a minor lie or something bigger, it can cause rifts and tremors in relationships. I think this is good as it promotes acceptance of others' betrayals and not being bitter about them as it can stifle your growth.

What is betrayal?
It's like stale food that you have been forced to eat;
It's like a sudden stab that you did not see coming;
It feels like cold water suddenly being poured
on your face without warning;
If trust were a human being,
betrayal would take it for a fool.

What is betrayal?
The more trusting you are of a person,
the deeper the impact of their betrayal;
The more time and energy you invest in a relationship,
the more painful the betrayal feels;
The more vulnerable you are with someone,
the more damaging their betrayal;
The more you try lowering your standards in order to fit in,
the angrier you get when betrayed;
The more you become aware of your lack of caution
and denial of signals from someone,
the more depressed you are when the betrayal occurs.

What is betrayal?
It happens when a person acts against you,
So, you do not have control over it;
It is solely dependent on the person who chooses to betray,
and there is nothing you can do to stop it;
It stems from emotions such as anger and jealousy,
or when someone is unhappy with your happiness;
You won't always know when the betrayal occurs,
only the one who betrays you knows the time and date.

What is betrayal?
The person who betrays you aims to satisfy their selfish desires
in order to move to the next stage;
To a betrayer, the act of betrayal is the norm;
Their acts follow a pattern,
and if you dig deep into their history,
you might find a chronology of betrayals and their victims.

If someone has betrayed you,
it means you have something they wish they had;
To some betrayers, you are just a means to their next achievement
– just a means to an end!

If you have been betrayed,
you are one of the few pacesetters in life
and have unique value.

Be kind to yourself when someone betrays you,
Find a counsellor or someone with a reliable track record
to discuss your pain and disappointment.

Remember, each betrayal feels dissimilar,
So, yours might be different;
Regardless, be kind to yourself.

Rain

I think the metaphor of rain is perfect for life. Life can be the perfect storm of good and bad. Likewise, it can be overwhelming and unbearable, but you must continue to fight against the 'rain' in anticipation of sunny days ahead.

Just as the rain that comes down from the sky,
It is inevitable that you will be hurt at one point in life,
And just as you cannot control the rain,
You can't control how other people will treat or react to you.

Sometimes, the strength of the wind overturns your umbrella,
Sometimes, you forget to take your umbrella along,
Sometimes, you are unable to get hold of it
before the rain starts,
Sometimes, wear and tear suggests that
it's time to replace it soon.

But, just as none of these reasons
causes you to stay indoors forever,
We, too, must learn to manage or seek support
for the hurt life throws at us.

Oil Of Truth

This is almost like a proverb in poem form. The idea of oil and water shows that regardless of how much you try to hide the truth, it will always rise above all. It is better to show your shortcomings and imperfections to people because the truth will always come out eventually. Being deceitful will only bring pain and problems.

Truth is like oil and lies like water,
No matter the amount of water you add to oil;
Mix them together all you like,
Oil will always float above.

So it is with truth,
No matter how much you try to cover it up,
The truth will always emerge;
Far sooner than you expect,
It will come out on top.

Your innocence will rise above the accusations,
So, get ready to float!

Forgive

This is a poem about choosing to forgive but not forget. Choosing to be burdened by someone's mistake can stifle your growth.

Be like a breeze in the way you forgive
and before you know it
you have forgiven the person who offended you.

Be like a chalkboard in the way you forgive,
Sometimes you hurt too much,
and sometimes, you forgive quickly.

Be like a pencil in the way you forgive
and erase the wrongs of others easily.

Be like a pen in the way you forgive
and you'll have a diary of wrongs you can revisit.

Be like a tattoo in the way you forgive,
Always refer to the wrongs as if they happened yesterday.

Be like an email in the way you forgive
and you'll have an archive of wrongs
accessible to later generations.

Be like WhatsApp in the way you forgive
and spread the remembrance of toxic wrongs to others.

Be like a sculptor in the way you forgive
and you will immortalise the wrongs for all spectators to
see, know, and remember
as long as the sculpture lasts.

Be like a highlighter in the way you forgive
and each time you see or remember the person,
you place their offence above their positive qualities.

Be like a candle in the way you forgive
and the offence becomes part of your identity.

Be like the sun in the way you forgive
and your countenance will reflect your forgiveness.

One-Member Family

One-member family!
How do I describe a one-member family?
Orphaned by default?
Late father and absent mother?
Or absent father and abandoned by mother?
Raised by an extended family, family friends or foster carers?
Raised differently from half-siblings?
struggling to connect?

Aunties and uncles say,
'You are our child, and we are here for you',
Yet, nature makes them put their own children's needs
before yours;
Making you feel second best,
Making you feel like everyone's child,
and nobody's daughter or son!

One-member family!
You try to fit in with your cousins
to become an accepted member of their nuclear family.
But, once again,
nature makes them prefer their own siblings above you.

Oh, one-member family!
How you desire to experience a sense of belonging
for once in your life;

You try to recreate your own family
with your friends and family network;

You give so much of yourself,
Sometimes you allow people to take advantage of you
Just so that you can be accepted!

You struggle to trust people from unfair experiences,
affecting your ability to connect;
You turned your zeal to work or addiction
to drown your desire for belonging,
But work or addiction could not fill the gap.

Oh, one-member family!
At what cost do you desire this sense of belonging?
Oh, what price are you ready to pay to eradicate your loneliness?

NONE!

So, who do we blame, humans or nature?
I know it can be lonely and routinely boring
being a one-member family,
But listen,
No one can fill that gap in you,
or bring a sense of wholeness;

You see,
Whether you are a one-member family or a five-member one,
What is important is that you are happy with who you are.

In the end you will realise that being a one-member family
is not a curse or burden,
It is just another type of family!

So raise your head high,
Straighten your shoulders
and walk like a celebrity because
YOU ARE ALL THAT MATTERS!

This poem will not apply to everyone.
However, if you are experiencing loneliness and it is impacting your well-being,
please seek help.

Use Your Grief

Words cannot express how much I will miss Liam,
but I believe he has gone to a better place.

Liam would sing my name to songs,
like the Hallelujah chorus.
Liam was the only one who would always say
how much I meant to him as a daughter,
each time we spoke over the phone,
or when we met face-to-face.

Liam loved being the centre of attention,
people fussing over him;
He loved company and bossing people around too.
He also had a wicked sense of humour.

My message to everyone today is
if you've ever lost a parent
and there's a longing for a father/mother figure,
just find an elder in your society to love and care for,
just as I did with Liam,
And if you're an older person longing to have a family,
or a child/parent relationship,
just look for a younger adult
and be a parental figure to them by loving them.

Love doesn't cost much,
it only requires time and dedication.

I really miss Liam,
for the love, care and fatherly attention he showered on me;
I also miss him
for the numerous times he would call in one day.

Love you lots and rest well.

(A tribute to a father figure who recently passed away)

Uniqueness

A concise piece with a clear message of acceptance and to own your unique features. The pressure to fit in as a young person is very high. These words, simply telling you to embrace your quirks, is a great message.

Just as our voices differ, so do our personalities,
As our talents differ, so do our temperaments,
As the texture of our hair varies,
so do our levels of tolerance.

As people age in different ways,
So, we all mature at different speeds;
As the sound of our cries differ,
So, does the nature of our strengths.

In diversity exists the path to invention,
In diversity, effective teamwork can be achieved,
In diversity lies healthy competition, not jealousy;
In diversity lies the spirit of one accord,
and respect for uniqueness.

I am me, and you are you,
So, we must all learn to embrace each other's
UNIQUENESS.

Busyness

This poem shows how you can get caught up in the busyness of life. How the repetition of mundane everyday tasks can cause your life to stagnate instead of grow. It shows that sometimes you need to take care of yourself and rest rather than fill your life with monotonous tasks.

Busyness, when it becomes a pattern,
makes me less efficient.

Busyness, when it becomes a pattern,
makes 'Always-Late' my middle name.

Busyness, when it becomes a pattern,
makes me live for others and neglect myself.

Busyness, when it becomes a pattern,
makes me disregard my health.

Busyness, when it becomes a pattern,
makes me bottle up my feelings.

Busyness, when it becomes a pattern,
makes me feel worn out.

Busyness, when it becomes a pattern,
makes me a person of all trades and a master of none.

Busyness, when it becomes a pattern,
makes me irritable for no good reason.

Busyness, when it becomes a pattern,
makes me assimilate less.

Busyness, when it becomes a pattern,
makes me grow insecure about my confidence.

Being a people-pleaser makes you busy, doesn't it?

Forced Marriage

This little snippet speaks volumes. Many people think that they will live a fairy-tale life once married. So they marry whomever they stay with the longest. The foundation of marriage should be love, how much you elevate each other to new heights, and the quality of the relationship. It shouldn't be based on co-dependency or the idea that all your problems will disappear.

Marriage is not a necessity,
Marriage is not the fulfilment of destiny,
Marriage does not free you from sadness,
Marriage does not meet all your needs,
Marriage does not warrant genuine respect,
Marriage does not make you whole;
Marriage based on love is a valid desire,
But being forced to get married is not.

---

*This poem will not apply to everyone,
but if you are a victim of forced marriage or about to become one, please seek help.*

My Partner

This poem shows that it's okay to be picky when looking for a partner. If you are going to spend most of your life with someone, it is an important criterion that you choose your partner wisely. The idea of a partner means equal responsibility in the marriage, which simply means they should be compatible with your version of marriage and vice versa.

I want a best friend, not an acquaintance;
I want a helpmate, not a business partner;
I want a partner to love and cherish, not a bedmate;
I want a role model to look up to, not a dictator;
I want a partner who will not take me for granted;
I want a partner with whom I can fulfil my potential;
I want a playmate with whom I can be foolish and vulnerable,
Without any fear of condemnation or rejection.

I want to marry my number one supporter,
A partner who will believe in me against all odds;
I want a partner who still finds me stunning
in my later years;
I want to marry for love, not reproduction;
I want to marry a partner I respect,
Whose advice I can take,
And not just a provider of basic needs.

I want to marry a partner who shows me love
And not just talks about it;
I want to marry a partner who is truly in love with me,
One who will love and protect me
in the face of shame, adversity, or calamity.

I want a partner for whom I can do all the above;
Here is my vision for marriage,
What's yours?

What Do You Do?

This poem is all about facing adversity. Although you may not have answers for the people who question you, eventually, you will be able to silence them when you become successful.

What do you do
when the one you look up to looks down on you?
What do you do
when the one you seek a solution from
is the source of the problem?
What do you do
when the one you trust rejects you?
What do you do
when the ones you thought were good
turn their back on you?

The thought of preventing my critics
from having the last laugh
motivates me not to give up,
I will keep on pressing on
until I silence my critics with my success.

I am pregnant with success
and I will not give it away in the face of opposition.

RISE

I have conceived a dream
therefore, I will deliver my vision.

Once my dream becomes a reality,
I will forget the pain of rejection.
Until then, I will continue to speak positively
about myself and my dream,
I will keep working hard,
knowing that perseverance will see me through;
That's what I will do.

Variety In Life

Things happen in life that no one can change. In a negative light, when this happens, it can cause great grief and pain. Although it's hard to look back at pain, it usually brings a large source of life lessons from which to learn. Though it is very important to look back at the past, please do not dwell on it, as it can stunt your growth in the future.

When you have seen war and fought in the battles of life,
Every moment of peace and joy feels like
a drop of water in a parched desert.

Unaddressed hurt will make you react
to anything that resembles such a hurt in life,
even when it is only a mirage.

Don't spend your life grieving
over something you cannot change.

Never let your worth be defined
by what is out of your control.

Never grow frustrated when you lack the power
to change, secure, or reproduce things;
Seek help instead.

Never let your life be defined by what it is missing,
Never base your life on trends because they change.

The greatest injustice you can cause yourself
is sacrificing what can be accomplished today
over the grief of something that happened yesterday.

Looking back and moving forward is never easy,
Neither is focusing on your past
while working on your future.

Days are like the wind:
Be careful how you spend yours,
for they do not return.

The value of a gift depends on the giver.

In the face of conflict,
It is easier to forgive someone who never said hurtful words
than someone who did.

You never outgrow encouragement.

Problems are like flowers:
They blossom one season, but eventually wither away.

Want to make a difference?
Don't dwell on the negatives of your past.

Ambitions:
Work on them one by one.

Never experiment with a new route,
Especially when you are running late for an appointment.

Ignorance sometimes breeds abuse,
so acquire knowledge.

Do not advise me on how to resolve a problem
when you are its source.

Lasting change never comes by force,
It comes through dialogue and negotiation.

The Love of My Unborn Children

The powerful message behind this piece is to seek what motivates you (the unborn child) in your darkest hour. It also encourages you to take a look at the accomplishments that have littered your turmoil, no matter how big or small. Finally, it lends the idea of being thankful, as some people would be happier with less. It is extremely easy to get weighed down in times of depression and sadness.

The love of my unborn children
Sent me back to school to achieve
A 2.1 Grade Point Average, against all odds;

The love of my unborn children
Motivates me not to give up on life,
Even when it seems to give up on me;

The love of my unborn children
Empowers me to fight for my rights,
Not surrender my will,
And to contribute to society;

The love of my unborn children
Leads me to discover strength
Even in nature's limitations;

The love of my unborn children
Steadies my hand from taking my life
And persuades me to carry on;

The love of my unborn children
Pushes me to fight back and press forward,
Even when I'm written off because of my disability,
Or delayed accomplishments;

The love of my unborn children
Reminds me always to love and pray for people,
Even when their attitude towards me is negative;

The love of my unborn children
Prompts me to measure the cost of decisions made
When tired, battered, and feeling defeated,
Lest I make an irreversible mistake;

The love of my unborn children
Keeps me holding on to a thread of hope
Until that hope is fulfilled.

Who are my unborn children?
They are the lives I've been privileged to care for,
motivate, empower, impact, and help reach their full potential

Life is hard,
but I choose to be harder on life by not giving up!
Why? Simply for the love of my unborn children.

Negatives

These words show that negatives can come in forms that may not reveal their true intentions. I think the similes of emotions evoke that. It shows that these can be the foundations of the destruction of a good character. Even though the poem focuses on the negatives people might endure, the last line shows there is a metaphorical light at the end of the tunnel; beyond the overbearing feeling of negativity, there is something positive to look forward to.

Peer pressure is like greed,
leading you to covet what is not rightly yours,
It doesn't reveal the consequences of your actions initially;
You only get to know them after.

Anger is like fire,
burning everything in its way;
Its damage is sometimes irreversible,
burning valuables beyond recognition.

Lies are like frogs,
adapting to changing temperature;
It is only a matter of time before
their survival is compromised.

Hopelessness has a suffocating stench,
overpowering the smell of other things;
It speaks of the death of dreams,
if left forever unchecked.

Pride is the murderer of good character,
killing your true self,
Thereby reducing you to a shell of yourself.

Unforgiveness is like cancer,
slowly eating you up from within;
It spreads to other people and hurts them with its bitterness.

Worry is a bully,
whispering falsehoods to you,
making claims about failure and impossibility;
The truth it tries to hide.

And while weeping might endure for a night,
Joy shall arrive at first light.

Words

*Sometimes, it's not **how** you say it but **what** you say. This poem shows how different words and language can dictate the response received. Therefore, it is important to carefully choose your language depending on the recipient of the message.*

Words are like a ghost,
So be careful what you call into your life
and the lives of others.

Bad or bitter words are like a contagious disease;
you might not sense the infection immediately.

Hurtful words are like tattoos
forcefully made on the heart of the listener.

Where there is strife,
even a shadow is interpreted as offensive.

Communication and clarification
are powerful tools for resolving conflict.

There's a message in every response;
Find it, and you will understand the response.

The word 'no'
will save you from living life as a people-pleaser;
The word 'please'
will make others go the extra mile for you;
The word 'sorry'
will make you the friend of multitudes;
The words 'thank you'
will open doors of opportunity for you.

Above all, these words aren't spells cast on the recipient,
These words will not always unlock the keys to success;
If these words do not bring positive change,
Be true to yourself, and success will follow.

Conscientious Awareness

A short poem that talks about listening to the voice of your conscience; it can be the moral compass in your life that empowers you to do good.

Conscientious awareness,
How powerful is your presence,
and how quiet is your voice.

Your constant whispers lead some to repentance
While others harden their hearts to drown out your voice.

How beautiful it is to have you as a best friend,
How wonderful it is to listen to you
and follow your lead.

How dreadful and dangerous it is
to ignore and overlook you,
Or to have you as a stranger in my life;
It would then only be a matter of time
before I bring sadness to other lives.

O conscientious awareness,
leave me not, or I will suffer!

Speak to me daily so that my life might bring
hope, joy, and faith to others.

My conscience,
Please remain my conscientious awareness,
and never leave me.

I Find

This short poem shines light on the power of positive thinking in negative situations. It begins with a negative, showing how we so often focus on the negatives within ourselves. However, it quickly spins into a positive, revealing even more positives. This shows that even though we focus on the negatives in our lives, we can find an equal, if not more, number of positives that we can be thankful for, regardless of the situation.

In my lack I find my gifts,
In my gifts I find my healing,
In my healing I find my strength,
In my strength I find my ministry,
In my ministry I find my imagination,
In my imagination I find my passion,
In my passion I find my invention,
In my invention I find my destiny,
In my destiny I find my success,
In my success, I find my fulfilment.

Poems Dedicated To Raising Awareness for Invisible Disability

Every Disability Matters

This piece highlights how so many disabilities can be hard to place without a physical focal point to show. This results in the foundation to succeed being limited when specific needs cannot be catered for. It shows that the path to success can often be like a house of cards; without the vital foundational pieces in place, such as the mentioned support, it can collapse. This is why it is our civic duty to put all these foundations in place to give everyone, regardless of background, an equal opportunity to succeed.

Invisible disability is like the air and wind:
Although you can't see them, you can feel their impact.

As the absence of air is suffocating to humans,
So is limited or lack of reasonable adjustments
for those with invisible disabilities who need support.

Reasonable adjustment comprises
equipment and/or non-equipment support,
Support sessions and, most importantly,
An invisible-disability-friendly workplace,
And management that can manifest an inclusive
and equal work environment.

Life without oxygen is crushing and constricting,
Similar to the lack of support for people
with invisible disabilities;
Both eventually result in death,
One physically, and the other in terms of losing employment
due to limited or the lack of support for such persons to excel.

A particularly reasonable adjustment for one
might not be the same for another with a similar disability;
Reasonable adjustments are not permanent,
They can change with a person's changing role,
Or as a new task is added to their duties.

Employers' ignorance, limited awareness,
And a lack of acceptance of the full impact
of the invisible disability on the individual,
Consciously or unconsciously,
Limits their access to the right support systems.

Hence, reasonable adjustments,
An invisible-disability-friendly environment
and management enables such people
to turn natural limitations into strengths.

This allows them to reach their full potential
and contribute effectively to society
via their chosen career path.

Employed & Disabled
~ I Can't Breathe! ~

Simply wow! ~Anonymous

Employed & Disabled – I Can't Breathe!

When you deny me access to reasonable adjustment,
When you decide what reasonable adjustment is best for me
without consulting me,
When I suddenly find myself in the hot seat
of a poor performance procedure
and I am still denied access to reasonable adjustment;

When you refuse to consider the impact of my disability
and the importance of reasonable adjustment,
When you do not understand my disability
and refuse to learn about it,
When you use symptoms of my disability
to determine or judge that I am unfit for a job
without referring to reasonable adjustments.

Employed & Disabled – I Can't Breathe!

No access to reasonable adjustment
Equals no access to job satisfaction!

Restricting my duties only to my areas of weakness
does not bring out the best in me;
When you don't ask how effective
the recommended adjustment is,
And are quick to assess my performance;
When you restrict me to duties
that make me look incompetent before my peers,
All because you delayed my access to reasonable adjustment;
When facts in supervision reports are misinterpreted
to make me look incompetent;
When you don't allow the recommended transition period
for me to familiarise myself with the reasonable adjustment,
before putting me on a performance plan;

Half access to reasonable adjustment is equal to
no access to reasonable adjustment!

Employed & Disabled – I Can't Breathe!

When you judge me blindly for my disability;
When you put systems in place to de-skill me
and then blame me for poor performance;
When you are yet to get guidelines from Access to Work
on how I can be supported;

When the coping strategies
that I have learnt over the years to support myself
are ignored.

Employed & Disabled – Please Let Me Breathe!

Writing this has been liberating,
but please don't condemn me for speaking out;
Some of us feel like we can't breathe
because of our invisible disability.

Please help before I stop breathing,
Please help prevent future generations with disability
from experiencing that suffocating feeling;
I must speak up for I realise
my silence will one day result in indifference to life.

Please help stop this global pandemic
of inequality towards people with disabilities,
Uniting as one voice in defence of peace and respect,
we can make inclusion a reality, not a statistic.

Thank you for standing up for me
Tomorrow might bring another issue,
but with zero tolerance for injustice,
I believe we can make this world a better place.

Thank you, George Floyd, for inspiring me to speak up.
As your daughter says, 'Daddy changed the world';

Your death has indeed led to a fight
to make the world a better place,
Rest in peace, brother.

And to the hero who recorded
the brutality against George Floyd;
The world thanks you.
As one of the black lives, I thank you.
To me, you are one of the greatest influencers of our time;
THANK YOU!

This poem will not apply to everyone.
However, if you have experienced discrimination at work and it has impacted your well-being,
please seek help.

Poems Dedicated To My Colleagues in Social Services

Looked After Children and Leaving Care Team
~ Team Unusual ~

Isn't this unusual?

A team wherein
having a disability or illness
is not treated as a weakness but as a strength;

A team wherein
people are paid to do their job,
but go the extra mile and put in extra hours
just because they care;

A team wherein
happiness, joy, and laughter form the norm;

A team wherein
the staff place the needs of young people before theirs
to ensure they fulfil their full potential;

A team that
celebrates everyone's achievements, birthdays, and more,
and stands by those who mourn;

Isn't this unusual?

A team wherein
the staff have lunch together on most days,
and share leftovers;

A team wherein
everybody smiles frequently and cracks jokes,
regardless of their workload and life trials;

A team wherein
the managers follow an open-door policy,
regardless of their work deadlines;

A team wherein
some young people dread the thought of their case being closed,
and some still visit in times of difficulty for support;

A team that
I look forward to working with
the minute I wake up every morning.

GOODBYE, MY UNUSUAL TEAM!

Dean at 50!
~ Who is Dean? ~

Dean at 50! Who is Dean?

Dean is the 30-year-old handsome specialist practitioner
who excels in his area of expertise;

Dean is seen as the main caregiver
in the Looked After Children's team;

Dean uses his skills to ensure team bonding,
and active participation during team meetings;

Dean is the gentle soul who talks less
but can easily tell when people are under stress;

Dean is the creative genius
who describes peoples' personalities in a way
that makes them the centre of his poems;

Dean is the soft-spoken colleague
whose style of running team meetings
captures his colleagues' attention;

Dean is the observant colleague
who knows what most colleagues like
through careful observation;

Dean at 50! Who is Dean?

Dean is the fashion icon of the team
whose socks will brighten your day;

Dean is the humble gentleman
who often uses those words
rarely used in our modern-day:
'Thank you' and 'Sorry'.

Dean is an individual
every team needs for their survival;

Dean is a team-maker, a humorous man,
and an expert at icebreaking.

HAPPY BIRTHDAY, DEAN!

Jane, The Water

Water is a necessity in life
just as Jane is to the team;
Water is flexible and accessible
just as Jane is to the team.

Water can be as firm as ice or as soft as snow,
just as Jane is in dealing with complex cases;

Water is soothing when one suffers from thirst,
just as Jane is to troubled colleagues;

Water helps with a shower on a tiring day,
just as Jane's listening skills
when interacting with stressed parents;

Water takes on many forms,
Jane, the mother, friend, colleague, and generous giver;

Water could be as large as the sea and as small as a drop,
just as Jane's diverse social work skills;

Water brings harvest, food, and joy,
just as Jane's supply of free snacks to the team.

Show me a human that can do without water,
I will show you a famine-stricken community;

Jane, the water;
you will be greatly missed but forever remembered.
Thank you for being the water in our lives.

A Foster Carer

A foster carer…
has a heart of forgiveness,
employs a teachable approach,
is relentless in their pursuit to provide and care,
is dependable and trustworthy,
is hardworking and thoughtful.

A foster carer…
May bear many scars of rejection,
failures, and disappointment,
but refuses to give up on children.

A foster carer…
is strong-willed and gentle when caring for others;
is rare, but when found, must be held onto.

Who Is AKM?

AKM's presence in the team feels like a sunrise,
AKM's smiles settle any unrest around her,
AKM's generosity ensures there's surplus food for the team.

AKM's friendly manner
enables people to ask countless questions,
AKM's proven record of kindness
transcends the Access Team,
AKM's assertiveness and gentleness
help in advocating for children's rights.

AKM's beauty is ageless!

AKM's social work skills are so diverse
she is almost a master of all;
AKM's humble spirit makes her more approachable to others;
AKM's uniqueness reflects in her name,
sharing it with only one person in the whole world.

AKM, the duchess with brains and beauty;
It has been a privilege knowing you.
Thank you for being AKM,
You will be greatly missed!

A Letter To Coronavirus

Dear *Coronavirus*,

The moment you came into our lives, no one could ever have imagined you would take so much away. You took away hugging, sitting next to someone, or quietly whispering in someone's ear. The thought of getting close to someone outside of one's bubble has become dangerous. Even going to the hospital became scarier than usual.

No one ever thought the words 'essential travel' would come into existence, and we would not be seeing our friends, colleagues, neighbours, or other locals moving freely on the street.

No one thought that we would never see their lips move or we would have trouble identifying familiar faces on the road because we all look different with a mask on.

Whoever thought our schools would be closed and children would have to follow social distancing rules, or that the usual noises from crowded environments, such as playgrounds, high streets, markets, etc., the sight of rush hour traffic, the unique beauty of peak-time travel in public transport would be halted?

Oh, how I miss group lunches with my colleagues and spontaneous parties with family and friends, not to mention those unannounced visits, going to the pub for a drink after work, shopping, or just fantasising whilst window shopping for expensive stuff.

Oh, Coronavirus,
The fear you birthed made so many shop excessively, to the extent that toilet paper became a scarce commodity. I particularly feared the scarcity of having access to my Nigerian food, so I too was guilty of excessive shopping.

Oh, Coronavirus,
What have we done to make you do this to us? You transformed our beautiful way of living as humans.

Coronavirus, you killjoy!
You limited our chances of sharing physical joy, play-fighting with loved ones, attending weddings, naming ceremonies, graduations, parties, leaving do's, and all types of joyful occasions. Dancing together has become a mere memory.

As if that were not enough, only a limited number of people could attend funerals, which made closure impossible for those who could not attend. Some had to mourn alone because their bubble was the person who died. Friends and family could not visit and only communicated virtually, unable to give the hugs and comforting touches. You took away the moment of having silence in a room when someone is unable to express words of comfort, but their presence makes the bereaved understand that they feel their pain. Most, if not all, died alone.

Oh, Coronavirus,
How I wish I could sue you! How I wish a judge could sentence

you and lock you up for the crimes you have committed.

Shame on you, *Coronavirus*,

You will never be forgiven for the pain you have caused us.

As I write this, tears of appreciation roll down my cheeks. I will never have enough words to express my gratitude to you all. You have all shown that you care.

To the council staff, who redeployed themselves to frontline COVID response services, distributing food among residents who were locked up in their homes, as well as making countless referrals to Social Services, necessary for residents who were vulnerable, the elderly and unwell as well as those with mental health issues: *I Thank You!*

To the council staff who were racing around, shopping for residents, delivering supplies to their doors, answering the phone, doing overtime, and cancelling holidays to enable them to reach more residents; for staying open from morning to night, seven days a week (including bank holidays): *I Thank You!*

To the food banks and charities for giving free food and support to the most vulnerable. To the borough's furloughed and unemployed, selflessly volunteering by grocery shopping or just talking to people who were lonely and afraid. The Unity Cafe for its dedication to providing meals for those who could not. To my very own Social Work colleagues, Foster Carers, our beautiful British weather, which was constant. And to everyone else not mentioned; to all of you, *I Thank You!*

Oh, how can I forget my loved ones, my very own 'natural', essential, and frontline workers of family and friends, who would drop food or groceries and other items at my doorstep, not because I was vulnerable, but just because they are beautiful people and they love me: *I Thank You!*

Last but not least, I am so proud of all the scientists around the world working tirelessly on vaccines. I also remember the selfless people who volunteered to participate in trials before the vaccine was made available to the public. Because of you, there is light at the end of this tunnel. *Thank You All!*

Safia Khokhar and Coral Nathan, 2021, Pandemic Poems
Poems written by staff, volunteers, residents and children of employees from the Royal Borough of Kensington and Chelsea and the City of Westminster. (Contributions by 25 authors; Pg. 46 written by Eniola Oluwasoromidayo)

Conclusion

I was motivated to publish this book after working with some young people who hardly had any family or friend support while in care. I think about how they will cope after leaving care, especially when they go through challenging times and desire to speak to a friend or family member, not a professional. On the other hand, some might have a good family and friends' support network, but they still wish to handle challenging times on their own without involving a professional, friend or family member.

To such young people and everyone else, this book is my little gift to supplement your support system when you need one. Please seek help if you need further emotional support. Remember, you are a GIFT to the world, and I believe the world is excited to experience how you will use your natural gifts, skills and talents to make it a better place for the present and next generations.

I believe in you, and I know you are destined for greatness. Greatness is not in fame or wealth but in what makes you feel fulfilled. Life can be hard sometimes, but remember to be harder on life by not giving up on yourself.

I wish you all the best in life!

~ *Eniola Oluwasoromidayo*

About the Author

Eniola Oluwasoromidayo is a trained social worker passionate about supporting children and young people in foster care or independent living, enabling them to settle and thrive in their aspirations. She also has a deep passion for helping people with neurodiversity, being neurodivergent herself.

Eniola lives in London, UK and is an advocate for counselling and therapeutic support.

If you would like to book Eniola Oluwasoromidayo for virtual meetings, events, keynote speaking engagements and more, please contact her at **eniolaoluwasoromidayo@gmail.com**

Ingram Content Group UK Ltd.
Milton Keynes UK
UKHW010852100323
418370UK00004B/422